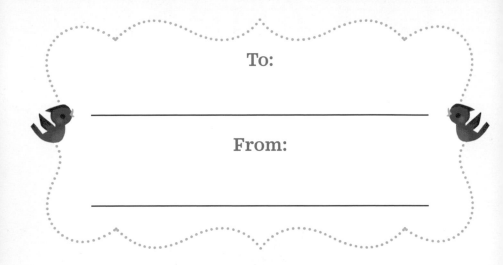

To:

_____

From:

_____

GROSSET & DUNLAP
An Imprint of Penguin Random House LLC, New York

Visit us online at www.penguinrandomhouse.com.

ISBN 9780593224908

10 9 8 7 6 5 4 3 2 1

THANKS

from
The Little Engine That Could®

illustrated by Jill Howarth

Grosset & Dunlap

Thankful for bright
morning sunrises,

and the kindness of friends.

For the beauty of the journey,

and good advice along the way.

Thankful for smiles
on rainy days,

and the laughs we share together.

For our incredible adventures,

and all the sights we see.

Most of all, thankful for you...

for cheering me on . . .

for making me feel loved . . .

and always reminding me to dream.